Space Invaders

Space Invaders

★ A Novel ★

Nona Fernández

Translated from the Spanish by Natasha Wimmer

Graywolf Press

The translation of *Space Invaders* is published by arrangement with Ampi
Margini Literary Agency and with the authorization of Nona Fernández and
Alquimia Ediciones.

This publication is made possible, in part, by the voters of Minnesota through
a Minnesota State Arts Board Operating Support grant, thanks to a legisla-
tive appropriation from the arts and cultural heritage fund. Significant support has also been provided by Target, the McKnight Foundation, the Lannan
Foundation, the Amazon Literary Partnership, and other generous contribu-
tions from foundations, corporations, and individuals. To these organizations
and individuals we offer our heartfelt thanks.

MINNESOTA
STATE ARTS BOARD

CLEAN
WATER
LAND &
LEGACY
AMENDMENT

TARGET.

Published by Graywolf Press
250 Third Avenue North, Suite 600
Minneapolis, Minnesota 55401

All rights reserved.

www.graywolfpress.org

Published in the United States of America

ISBN 978-1-64445-007-9

2 4 6 8 9 7 5 3 1
First Graywolf Printing, 2019

Library of Congress Control Number: 2019931354

Cover design: Walter Green

Lettering: Camryn Mothersbaugh

Cover art: ESA (European Space Agency) / Hubble & NASA, RELICS

For Estrella González J.

I am at the mercy of this dream:
I know it's just a dream
but I can't escape it.

Georges Perec, *La boutique obscure*

Space Invaders

First Life

I

Santiago de Chile. 1980. A ten-year-old girl walks into an Avenida Matta school holding her father's hand. A leather satchel hangs on one shoulder and the laces of her right shoe are undone. Outside, the sidewalk is strewn with the remains of a celebration: flyers, empty bottles, trash. The new constitution proposed by the military junta was approved by a broad majority. The school caretaker sweeps the litter from the gate, watching the girl's father. The man takes off his officer's cap to say good-bye to his daughter. He gives her a kiss on the cheek and whispers a few words in her ear. The girl smiles and heads down the hallway with one shoelace trailing on the tiles. In front of the statue of the Virgen del Carmen she kneels and kisses her thumb.

II

Sometimes we dream about her. From our far-flung mat-
tresses in Puente Alto, La Florida, Estación Central, or San
Miguel, from the dirty sheets that mark our current location,
tucked away on cots that cradle our tired bodies that work
and work; at night, and sometimes even during the day, we
dream about her. The dreams are all different. Different as
our minds, different as our memories, different as we are and
as we've become. Amid all our oneiric differences, we agree
that we see her as we each remember her, in our own way.
Acosta says that in his dream she's a girl, the way she was
when we met her, in her school uniform, her hair pulled back
in two long braids. Zúñiga says no, she never wore her hair
in braids. He sees her face framed by long, thick black hair,
hair that only he remembers, because Bustamante sees her
another way, and so does Maldonado and so does Riquelme
and so does Donoso, and each and every vision is different.
Hairstyles and colors vary, her features never quite come
into focus, shapes blur, and there's no way to agree, because
in dreams, as in memory, there is no agreement, nor should
there be.

Fuenzalida dreams about the first time she saw her.
When she wakes up she can't remember what her hair looked
like, so she doesn't debate that with the rest of us, because,
to Fuenzalida, what matters in dreams are voices, not hair.
Fuenzalida dreams about many children's voices whispering

7

in the fifth-year room, and about the teacher taking attendance. Acosta—here, Bustamante—here. The voice of each child sounds exactly as it did back then, because even though voices fade with time, dreams have the power to bring them back to life. Donoso—here, Fuenzalida—here. And then it's her turn, her name uttered from beneath the teacher's black mustache. González, we hear in the classroom; and from the desk in the very back row where she sits alone, the new pupil—or maybe not so new—says *here*. It's her. Nothing else matters, not the style of her hair, the color of her skin or her eyes. Everything is relative except for the sound of her voice, because in dreams, according to Fuenzalida, voices are like fingerprints. González's voice seeps into us from Fuenzalida's dreams, invading our own visions, our own versions of González, settling in and keeping us company night after night. Some nights it visits Acosta's pillow, or Donoso's torn sheets. And so the nightly rounds are a never-ending roll call, an eternal head count that disturbs our peaceful sleep. Years have passed. Too many. Our mattresses, like our lives, have been scattered around the city, have drifted apart. What has become of each of us? It's a mystery that scarcely needs solving. We share dreams from afar. Or one dream, at least, embroidered in white thread on the bib of a checkered school smock: Estrella González.

III

They've arranged us in a long single file line down the middle of the schoolyard. Next to us is another long line, and then another, and another. We form a perfect square, a kind of game board. We're pieces in a game, but we don't know what it's called. We spread out, each of us resting a right arm on the shoulder of the classmate ahead to mark the perfect distance between us. Our uniforms neat. Top button of the shirt fastened, tie knotted, dark jumper below the knee, blue socks pulled up, pants perfectly ironed, school crest sewn on at the proper chest height, no threads dangling, shoes freshly shined. Displaying clean fingernails, ringless hands, bright faces, hair brushed into submission. Singing the national anthem every Monday first thing, each according to their ability, in piercing off-key voices, loud and almost bellowing voices enthusiastically repeating the chorus, as up front one of us raises the Chilean flag from where it rests in somebody else's arms. The little star of white cloth rising up, up, up till it touches the sky, the flag finally at the top of the staff, rippling over our heads in time to our singing as we stare up at it from the shelter of its dark shadow.

IV

Maldonado dreams about letters. They're old letters in the handwriting of ten-year-old girls. Letters that she and González used to mail to each other, as if they didn't see each other in the classroom every day, as if they were as far apart then as they are now. González's spelling isn't good, says Maldonado, but her writing is careful, neat. She's a different person in her letters, not the shy girl in the back row of the classroom. Maldonado's dreams are of reading each of these letters. Dreams built of words, assembled from letters and sentences. Names written in blue ball-point pen, addresses and signatures, and sincerely, and yours truly, and hugs, and write back soon, friends forever, swear you'll never forget me.

Fuenzalida says everybody dreams in their own way. So while she hears voices, and others see only pictures, Maldonado has every right to dreams constructed out of words. Each brick is a verb, an article, an adjective, and the frame goes up, stairs are built, the dream becomes a tall tunnel connecting heaven and hell. Maldonado dreams blue words in girls' handwriting. The most frequently repeated word is a name. It's written on the flap of the envelope and at the end of each letter. Beside it is the drawing of an inked-in star, like a kind of brand, an emblem fallen from some flag.

Dear Friend, hello! How are you and your family? Good, I hope. Because I have a cold and some other problems. Remember the letter you sent me? I never wrote back but I have to, because if I don't I'm not a good friend, and I think we're friends although sometimes in class you act like you don't know me. You're somebody I can trust. I have so much to tell you you won't believe it. Secret things, things I can't tell anybody except you, things I haven't even said or written or thought. Lots of things. Things that have nothing to do with Zúñiga or people teasing me about him. I don't care about him. The things I have to tell you are other things. More important things, secret things. But this paper is tiny and my writing is so big and fat. My dad says I have to write smaller and stay on the lines but the lines are so thin they're hard to see. If I listened to my dad I could write more but since I can't write small and stay on the tiny little lines I have to write less. I should try to obey my dad. He deserves to be obeyed, for me to obey him. Now he's at the National Police Hospital. Did you know that my dad had a work accident? Nobody at school knows. He's had lots of operations. That's why I have to try to write smaller like he says. And my mom has to stay in bed too, but at home. It's because she's going to have a baby, but this time is different. You know how my little brother Rodrigo died last year. He was only a year younger than me, so when I turn eleven he would have been ten. That's why mom and dad and I really want a new little brother. I think he'll be my baby too in a way. Do you want to have kids? When I'm grown up I want to have lots. I'm going to be a mom with lots of kids and what happened with Rodrigo won't happen to any of them. The Virgin will keep them safe. I have faith in her. And she'll keep my mom and the baby safe too. So I have to be good, that's just what I have to do. I have to finish my homework and try to write smaller. I hope you get good grades on all our *exams. Did you know that August 12 was my dad's birthday? Well now I have to end this letter because if I don't I'll have to think of something else to say and I don't know what else to say and this paper is small and my writing is big and fat and there's no more room.*

Bye, Maldonado, my friend.
I hope you like my tiny little letter.
Write back soon.

Your classmate, ★

P.S. What you said about Zúñiga is true. But I only like his hair and his eyes, because the rest of him is dark and ugly.

V

Riquelme dreams of spare hands. The hands from González's house. Riquelme is the only one of us who ever went there, so his dreams are like testimony. Riquelme says that the house was big and dark and full of closed doors. Behind one of the doors was González's brother's room. You couldn't go in there. Behind two other doors on the second floor, up a staircase with no railing, were González's bedroom and her parents' bedroom. You could go in there, but he didn't. No one asked him to. Downstairs there was a dining room and a living room and a den with a TV and an Atari set that used to belong to González's brother but that now belonged to González and was okay to use. Riquelme and González played *Space Invaders* for hour after hour. The green glow-in-the-dark bullets of the earthlings' cannons scudded up the screen until they hit some alien. The little Martians descended in blocks, in perfect formation, shooting their projectiles, waving their octopus or squid tentacles, but González and Riquelme had superpowers, and the aliens always ended up exploding. Ten points for each Martian in the first row, twenty for the ones in the second row, and forty for the ones in the back row. And when the last one died, when the screen was blank, another alien army appeared from the sky, ready to keep fighting. They gave up one life to combat, then another, and another, in a cycle of endless slaughter. Projectiles flew back and forth. González and Riquelme killed as many Martians as they could, but despite their efforts, they couldn't match the record that González's brother had set a year ago. It was a high score, tough to beat. No matter how hard they tried that afternoon in their battle against the aliens, they couldn't break the record.

After a while González's mother, Doña González, brought them milk and said they had to do their homework. They had a history assignment on the War of the Pacific, Chile's never-ending battle with Peru and Bolivia. González and Riquelme sat at the table in the dining room and got to work. Riquelme doesn't remember much about what they did, but he does remember the sopapillas with powdered sugar that Doña González brought them and the photograph of González's brother hanging on the wall. According to Riquelme, González's brother looked a lot like González. Like a male copy of her. Riquelme wanted to ask what had happened to him, but he was afraid to. Hanging next to the picture of González's brother were some medals with tricolor ribbons, the kind won by athletes or soldiers. There were copper plaques and there were cloth and metal mini flags, lots of them. Flags that might be used in an assignment about the War of the Pacific, or to conquer some Martian territory.

That's what Riquelme was doing, looking at González's brother and the medals hanging on the wall, when González's father, Don González, came in. Riquelme had never met him before. Few of us had. He was a big man in uniform who was always traveling and could occasionally be seen dropping González off at school in the morning. That afternoon—as usual, most likely—Don González kissed his wife and his daughter and gave Riquelme a friendly nod. Then, after he had greeted everyone and as if it were something he did every day, like someone loosening his tie and settling in for the evening, Don González sat in a chair and took off his left hand. It was a wooden hand, like the peg leg of a pirate. There was a black leather glove on it.

González's mother saw that Riquelme was uncomfortable. Quickly she ushered her husband and his wooden hand upstairs. González explained to Riquelme that there had been a terrible accident and that that was how her father had lost his left hand. Another national police officer happened to pick up a bomb, and somehow the pin got pulled. To save the officer's life, Don González did something, nobody knows exactly what, but he grabbed the bomb with his left hand, poor little hand, and tried to throw it far away, and before he could, the bomb went off. Every night when he got home, he took off the prosthesis that he wore where his poor little hand should be, because prostheses pinch and you can't wear them for too long. He had lots of them, she said, and he kept them in a special cabinet. All made out of wood, either beech or larch, and all made to his precise measurements, so that he wouldn't miss his left hand, poor little hand.

Riquelme never went back to González's house. The thought of those orthopedic hands terrified him. The few times he and González were partners on an assignment, he would invite her to his apartment, where hands didn't come off bodies and children didn't hang on the wall. The rumor spread around the school like a kind of myth, and no one, absolutely no one, dared to go over to her house for fear of Don González's spare hands. Not even Maldonado, who exchanged letters with González, and who claimed to be her best friend. People said that there were steel hands and silver hands and bronze hands. Someone said that Don González had a hand that could shoot bullets and another hand that could stab you, because knives popped out of it. Razor-sharp fingers, 2.5-caliber fingernails, cannon hands or guillotine hands.

Now Riquelme dreams about that never-seen cabinet full of prostheses and about a boy playing with them, a boy he never met. The boy opens the doors of the cabinet and shows him the orthopedic hands lined up one after the other, orderly as an arsenal. They're glow-in-the-dark green, like the *Space Invaders* bullets. The boy gives a command and the hands obey him like trained beasts. Riquelme feels them exit the cabinet and come after him. They menace him. They chase him. They advance like an army of earthlings on the hunt for some alien.

VI

We button our smocks, checkered for girls and tan for boys.
One button after the other, carefully, so that no buttonhole
is missed, the same action six times, from the neckline at the
top to the hem at the bottom. When we're ready, we take our
places next to our wooden desks. We stand one after the
other in a long line across the classroom. Next to ours is
another long line, and another, and another. We are mul-
tiple columns forming a perfect square, a kind of game
board. With our right hands, we cross ourselves at the same
time, looking up at the picture of the Virgen del Carmen
that hangs over the board, directly above our heads. It's
a small painting, slightly faded, but it's the lady with her
golden crown and a tricolor sash across her chest, with her
child in her arms, the little baby Jesus. In the name of the
Father, the Son, and the Holy Spirit, we recite a prayer to
the Virgin to begin the day and we pray for the poorest of
the poor, the wretched, the homeless, for those who aren't
able to go to school like we do. Voices in unison raised in
a prayer identical to yesterday's and the day before yesterday's and tomorrow's. *Virgencita*, our mother, and mother
of the Savior, lead us on a path of peace, on a path free of
fears and dangers, through a life of light and fulfillment,
far from the hardships and terrors of the world. Forsake us
not in doubt, heavenly mother, abandon us not in suffering,
and grant us the joy of your eternal kingdom, sweet mother,

blessed in all things, forever and ever. Amen. A kiss on the thumb in conclusion and then we take our wooden seats to begin whatever class it is, under the protection of the Virgin, who watches us from on high. She always watches us from on high. Her glass eyes spying on us over our neatly combed heads.

VII

We're in a ship made of colored paper. It's a big ship, with a crew of thirty-four sailors, who are us, all under the command of an us, who is Zúñiga, the captain. His mother has painted a black beard on him with burnt cork and dressed him in a sailor suit, which is just his blue school coat trimmed with yellow construction paper. Music blares from a record player as González, who is the tallest of the sailors, who are us, holds the Chilean flag and waves it in time to the music. Zúñiga thinks she looks pretty dressed like a man. She has burnt-cork whiskers too, and a little white sailor hat, like we all do. Zúñiga is looking at her. We all notice, except for her. Gentlemen, we are outmatched, says our captain and we gaze at him with patriotic eyes. But be brave and take heart. Our flag has never fallen in the face of the enemy and I hope that this day will be no different. While I live, the flag will fly, and if I die, my officers know their duty. Long live Chile, damn it, concludes Zúñiga, and he sets out to board the enemy ship.

I'm a hero. Every year, on May 21, it's my job to be one. I don't know why they choose me, I don't look like Arturo Prat, but I'm as brave as he was and I'm just as willing to die for something or someone. Year after year I take part in this perpetual disaster that, it seems, will never end. In a moment of déjà vu, it's my turn to die again on the enemy deck for my country and my honor. Just like last year, and the year before, and the year before that. I leave my ship of colored paper, I leap with my sword in my hand, but instead of dropping down onto the enemy ship, I land in the white sheet that is the sea. I don't land on the Peruvian ship that we built yesterday in the classroom. I don't do the thing I've practiced so many times.

I search for the teacher in the audience, but I can't find her. I want to explain that this isn't my fault. It's not that I don't want to go into battle, but the white sheet has snared me. I fall into it and it swallows me up and hides me and lulls me to sleep. I don't remember this white sheet. Someone put it here at the last minute. It wasn't part of the play. It wasn't part of this battle. I want to ask for help, but it wouldn't look good. I'm a hero, not a coward. And though I know I'm going to die anyway, I resist and try to raise my head from the sea of cloth. I see my sailors over there on the ship. All of them are waving their right hands at me. It looks like a farewell. González hasn't let go of the flag, she's holding it and she flaps it like a big handkerchief. She comes over to the railing. Her face is wet with drops of seawater that she dries with a corner of the flag. But now that I think about it, those drops might have been tears.

González is crying. They say her brother drowned. No one knows how or why. Maybe it was like this, wrapped in a white sheet like the sea. González tosses me the flag and I try to grab it. I pretend it's a life preserver. The flag covers me, like the sheet. I twist, I roll, I'm carried away by the current, I drown and I sleep. I sleep deeply. It seems to me that I die under the tricolor fabric.

I wake up.

She's sitting on my bed.

I feel the weight of her body close to mine.

Zúñiga, she says, you survived. I half hear her over the white noise of the television, which is still on. It's late. I know I'm dreaming, but her voice in my ear is as real as the feather weight of the sheets on my body. It's her. I can see her by the light of the television screen. Her black hair, the freckles on her nose, a white sailor hat and the burnt-cork mustache, smudged by her tears. You came back? I ask her and she smiles. Her hair smells faintly of gum. The television screen announces a new day's programming. It begins with the national anthem and pictures of the whole country from Arica to Punta Arenas.

I wake up again.

There's no television.

I'm alone and I've grown old.

Second Life

I

Santiago de Chile. 1982. The girl sits on a bench in the schoolyard, eating ham and cheese on a roll. Her seventh-year classmates run and play around her. A few months ago, ex-president Eduardo Frei Montalva, leader of the opposition to General Augusto Pinochet, died of unexplained septic shock at a private clinic. Soon after, operatives of the Central Nacional de Inteligencia shot union leader Tucapel Jiménez five times in the head before slitting his throat. Both stories made the headlines. Two copies of those newspapers are filed in the school library, in a fat binder on shelf number four in the third aisle. None of the children in the school have ever opened that binder. Now, in the schoolyard, the bell rings for the end of recess. The girl shakes the crumbs from her checkered smock and then rises. The children line up by grade. She joins her classmates and waits for a signal from the monitor to walk to her classroom. While she waits she looks at her red-painted nails. Her arm is on the shoulder of the classmate ahead of her, to mark the proper distance, and as she stands there she examines the polish, which has started to peel. The girl senses the gaze of the monitor inspecting the lines. Everyone begins to move forward, one after the other. The girl puts her hands in the pockets of her smock. No one notices.

II

Dear friend, hello! How are you? Did you like the postcard
I sent you from Germany? I wrote you what day and time I was
coming so that you could meet me at Pudahuel Airport but you
weren't there. Anyway we had a great time. Germany is big
and beautiful. We took lots of pictures and ate lots of sausages.
Germany is split in half by a wall. I only saw one side, the good
side, it's the only side you can visit because the other side is too
dangerous. My little brother was fine, we were all worried about
traveling with him, but nothing happened. He cried a little on
the plane, but babies cry so even though I was embarrassed my
mom told me it was normal. Moms aren't embarrassed when
their children cry. That's how I'm going to be with my babies.
The only terrible thing about the trip was that they operated on
my dad's ear. This is the fourth operation he's had so that part
was sad and we cried a little. He still hasn't recovered from his
terrible accident. But the doctors there are better and so they
sent him to Germany to have the operation. The trip back was
hard too because we had layovers, so the plane took off and
landed and his ear hurt every time we went up or down. But
I liked that because I got to see more places. I saw Paris, I saw
Spain, which is really nice, and the last stop was Rio de Janeiro
which was my favorite. I bought postcards, and I'll send them
to you one at a time when my uncle Claudio can take me to the
post office. Uncle Claudio is a new uncle. Basically I'm not al-
lowed to leave the house alone anymore so I have to go out with

Uncle Claudio, who is an uncle from my dad's work who takes care of me and comes with me when I go out, because my mom stays with my brother, my dad is at work a lot, and I can't be alone out of the house because it could be as dangerous as crossing to the other side of the wall in Germany. I'll go with him to the post office and I'll send you this letter which hopefully you'll answer very soon. On the trip I brought the letter you wrote me and I read it every night. I even showed it to my dad. Zúñiga wrote me a letter too but not by mail. He gave me a little rolled-up piece of paper before I left. It's not very long but I brought it with me too to remember him by. I didn't show his letter to my dad. He doesn't like Zúñiga, he says his family is strange. I didn't show it to my mom either because she says the same thing. I didn't show it to anybody. I'll show you later.

Do you know what my middle name is? Zúñiga doesn't know. I'll tell you. It's Marisella.

Alright, my dear friend Maldonado. I can't think of anything else to write.

Now I'm going to the post office with my uncle.

Sincerely yours.
Love. ★ Marisella.

III

*We don't know whether this is a dream or a memory. Some-*times we think it's a memory creeping into our dreams, a scene that escaped from one person's head, lurking in everyone's dirty sheets. It might have been lived once, by us or by someone else. It might have been staged or even made-up, but the more we think about it the more we're sure it's just a dream that gradually became memory. If dreams and memories were truly different, we might be able to identify its source, but on our memoryless mattresses everything is mixed-up and the truth is that it doesn't really matter anymore.

First it's me running with Riquelme along one of the second-floor corridors at school. Let's go, Zúñiga, he says as we hurry down the stairs, trying not to make a sound. We're heading for the front door. We have flyers in our pockets. Lots of flyers, a big pile. My hands are stained blue from the ink. We have to scatter them in front of the school without anyone seeing us. I'm not sure what they say; I guess it's something about a march, a call to a big march against Pinochet, something unheard-of, something new, something really important, because it was my big brother who asked me to do this and when he did he said that it was a mission for the bravest of the brave and that I'm a brave man, which means I can do this, and more. So we sneak out of class and we get past the caretaker and before the bell rings for the end of the school day, we open our bags and scatter the flyers in front of the school so that everybody will see them when they come out. Parents, guardians, drivers, teachers, neighbors, little kids and big kids, will be able to read them on the ground, pick them up, and bring the information home. Hunger march, say the blue mimeographed letters. Again and again on the ground. All those flyers for all to see. Hunger march on the sidewalk, hunger march at the bus stop, hunger march by the kiosk, hunger march by the public telephone. The mission is a success. No one has seen us, so we can return to school triumphant and when we get out of class my brother will see what a good job we've done, and he'll probably buy me some Chilean trading cards for my Spanish World Cup album.

When we're about to step back inside someone honks a horn at us. A red Chevy Chevette is parked out front. From inside a guy nods at us. He's a dark man, with a mustache, a big nose, a pair of dark glasses that hide his eyes. He's smoking a cigarette as he waits—because it looks like he's waiting for someone. I don't know him. I've never seen him before. Neither has Donoso, or Fuenzalida, or Bustamante. Riquelme has, though. He says it's González's uncle. A guy who drives her places, a relative or something. He brings her to school or wherever and then he takes her home. Maldonado says it's someone from her father's job, Don González's job. Maldonado says his name is Uncle Claudio and he's funny, he likes to kid around, and he let her smoke one of his cigarettes. Riquelme says that a week ago he came to pick González up at Riquelme's apartment after they had been working together on a science project with Acosta and Maldonado. He was sitting in Riquelme's dining room drinking a cup of tea and he talked for a long time to Riquelme's grandmother. Riquelme says he's nice, he promised to take Riquelme for a ride in the red Chevy whenever he wants. Probably he would let him smoke one of his cigarettes too. I've never been in a red Chevy. Neither has Riquelme. I once had a toy Chevy when I used to collect little cars. It was my favorite, but I don't know where it is now. It got lost. The man in the red Chevy smiles at us from the car holding one of the flyers we've just scattered. He must have picked it up from the ground. Hunger march in the clutch of González's Uncle Claudio. Riquelme nods back at him. I do too, though I don't know him. I even raise my hand. I have a secret fantasy that he'll take me for a ride in the red Chevy.

IV

The game is simple and we have an hour to play it. Everybody knows and that's why we all show up on time. Our mothers and fathers are in the parent meeting and we shut ourselves in here, in this dark classroom belonging to the grade above or the grade below, never our own classroom. We like to come at night, though we aren't invited. Our parents sit at our desks, answer to our names on the attendance list, and discuss things involving us with our teacher. Meanwhile, here, a few yards away, we've changed out of our uniforms and we're wearing other clothes, our own clothes, real clothes, ready to be real and play our own game.

The light is off in the classroom and the air thickens. Amid a darkness as black as night or death, we, the usual someones, stop being ourselves. Now no one is who they claim to be. No name is embroidered on the lapel of any smock. We're different people. Shadows, hushed ghosts moving silently with arms and hands outstretched, trying to run into something. Donoso goes after Maldonado. He touches her shoulder, then her neck, he tangles his fingers in a mop of hair that he thinks is hers. Bustamante finds an elbow that's connected to someone's right hand—whose hand he doesn't know, and he doesn't ask, either. Fuenzalida's face meets Riquelme's, nose to nose. They breathe together, registering each other's smell and taste, testing each other's saliva. Zúñiga moves around the dark room in search of González. He pats heads, legs, arms, and he wants to call out, but names don't work here, attendance-taking is left outside of the dark room, and González is no longer González, because now she's part Maldonado, part Fuenzalida, part Acosta too. And a tongue slips into Zúñiga's mouth. It's a little tongue, though very intrusive, a tongue that could be anyone's. And somebody laughs and somebody hides, and somebody laughs again, while someone else sneezes in a corner and someone collides with the chalkboard at the front of the room. Bustamante's ears are burning, he feels like he's about to burst. Donoso bites Maldonado's neck, apparently he can't help himself, and Maldonado howls like a cat. Zúñiga laughs because of the tickling, someone is tickling him or maybe no one is and it's just laughter, pure laughter that seizes us all, while the quartz watch with the little light on somebody's wrist counts down the minutes until the end. Then, in the last seconds of the game, come the clutches, the crushes, the squeezes, the tongues licking and seeking and not speaking, because here there are no words, no names, we're just one body with many paws and hands and heads, a little Martian from *Space Invaders*, an octopus with multiform arms playing this game in a darkness that's about to lift.

The light suddenly comes on and the monitor is watching us from the doorway. We're all exactly where we're supposed to be, boys to the right and girls to the left. Some are reading books. Others are asleep in their seats because it's late and tomorrow we'll have to get up early to come back to school.

V

Apparently Zúñiga and Riquelme did something terrible.
They were caught doing something, which is why they were
suspended for a few days, which is why they aren't here, says
Maldonado. Zúñiga got into politics, and that's why all of this
is happening to him, says Acosta. What do you mean he got
into politics? asks Donoso. He can't get into politics, he's too
young, says Maldonado. He can because his parents are re-
sistance leaders and his brother is in the resistance too, says
Fuenzalida. What does it mean to be in the resistance? asks
Donoso. Everybody in the upper school is a leader or a fighter
in the resistance. Get with it, we're not kids anymore, says
Bustamante. We are kids, says Maldonado, we're only twelve.
We're not, sometimes there's no such thing as too young, says
Bustamante. Anyway what is politics? Everything is politics.
So what's the point. Who cares. Basically there's a reason you
can't get political, there's a reason it's forbidden by the gov-
ernment. It isn't right for things to be forbidden. Who cares
about that shit. Don't swear. I'll talk however I want to talk.
Then I'll tell the monitor. You're probably the one who told
on Zúñiga and Riquelme. I didn't tell on anybody. I have no
idea what Zúñiga and Riquelme are up to. Does anybody
have any idea what Zúñiga and Riquelme are up to? Actually,
does anybody have any idea what it means to get into politics? Be quiet, here comes the math teacher. Everybody in
their seats, everybody sit down, everybody quiet. The door

is opening. Good morning, boys and girls. Time for attendance. Acosta, Bustamante, Donoso. Blah blah blah. Open
your books to page thirty-two. Teacher, before we start we
want to ask you a question. What's the question, what is it.
What does it mean to get into politics. How old do you have to
be. Silence. The teacher stares, startled. Silence. The teacher
hesitates before answering. Silence. Fuenzalida dreams of
him, of the silence that settled over the classroom, which she
can hear as clearly as our voices. Silence. No one says a thing,
not a seat creaks, not a sheet of paper rustles. Boys and girls,
says the math teacher, this is math class and you're here to
learn, not to talk nonsense.

VI

Our little red toy Chevy crosses the schoolyard. It rolls past the statue of the Virgen del Carmen and turns at the corner of the soccer field on the way to the fountain. It bounces over some bread crumbs and past a few pebbles and an orange peel. Inside, from the backseat, we gaze out the window, smoking a couple of cigarettes. In this dream we're tiny too, the size of the red Chevy, so we can do whatever we want because nobody can see us down here. We can paint our nails, roll down our socks, loosen our ties, take off our smocks. If we want to we can even let down our hair and hold hands. The monitor walks past. We see his giant black shoe. His sole is about to crush us, but the tiny red Chevy dodges him in an incredible maneuver and saves us from being squashed to death by his loafer. The monitor doesn't even notice us, can't see us from above, doesn't suspect what we might be getting up to down here in the backseat of the red Chevy. In the front seat, González's uncle Claudio is at the mini steering wheel. He's tiny like us. He's the pilot of this dream, everyone's fantasy, driving the tiny car at top speed, swerving around obstacles in the schoolyard like a real race car driver. On the windshield of the red Chevy, held in place by the wipers, is a flyer with blue letters. Hunger march, we read, as González's uncle Claudio smiles at us in the rearview mirror.

VII

We've never done it before, but we're doing it. We're through the gate and we're walking out of school in a pack. We follow one after another in a long line, but instead of filing into the classroom, this time we're heading out. We move into place, each of us resting a right arm on the shoulder of the classmate ahead to mark the perfect distance between us. Our uniforms neat. Top button of the shirt fastened, tie knotted, dark jumper below the knee, blue socks pulled up, pants perfectly ironed, school crest sewn on at proper chest height, no threads dangling, shoes freshly shined. One step forward, then another, and another. We go marching, leaving the school behind, losing ourselves among buildings, buses, cars, office workers, street vendors, beggars. Eyes forward, gaze never dropping below shoulder height. Not retreating. Making our way through the center of the city, which embraces us. Alert to its movements, its smiles, the other people who join us along the way. Suddenly, in the middle of a broad avenue, two hands that aren't ours begin to clap to an unfamiliar beat. One and two. One and two. Other hands that aren't ours join in the clapping. One and two. One and two. And then, so as not to be outdone, we lift our hands from the shoulders of our trusty classmates and without knowing how, we've got it, one and two, beating out a new rhythm that seizes our bodies. Someone shouts something and someone repeats it. Somebody else shouts something and many others repeat it. We shout what's being shouted. We don't understand what it means, but that's what we do. We howl a howl that comes from somewhere that isn't our mouths, a chant invented and started by others, but made for us. One and two, one and two, our hearts beating in time to the words echoing off the buildings. Everybody clapping, the smell of sweat, of clothes washed in unfamiliar detergent, cigarettes, smoke, burnt rubber. And the line breaks apart. Acosta is separated from Bustamante and Donoso, and we lose Fuenzalida and Maldonado somewhere, as others crowd in between us. New uniforms appear, new school crests, new hairstyles, and the line gets longer, while next to us we see another long line, and beyond that another, and another. All of the columns forming a perfect and unbreakable square, a block that advances in lockstep, a single unit moving on the game board. We are the most important piece in a game, but we still don't know what game it is.

VIII

A green glow-in-the-dark hand. Riquelme keeps dreaming about it, can't shake it. This time he sees it on a television screen. The hand advances rapidly, in pursuit of extraterrestrial children. They run back and forth, fleeing in terror, but the hand clutches at the first Martian within reach and at its touch there is an explosion. The body of the little Martian flies apart into colored lights that vanish from the TV screen. On the screen the score goes up by one hundred points, but the amazing record set by González's brother stands unbroken. The green hand and many other green hands stream out of an earthling cannon, on the hunt for more space invaders.

Third Life

I

Santiago de Chile. 1985. On March 29, brothers Rafael and Eduardo Vergara Toledo, ages eighteen and twenty, respectively, are shot and killed by national police operatives in the working-class neighborhood of Villa Francia. Both had dropped out of school, under suspicion of being agitators and pamphleteers. That same day, at 8:50 a.m., in front of the Colegio Latinoamericano de Integración, Manuel Guerrero, a teacher, and José Manuel Parada, a parent, both communist militants, were kidnapped by the national police. Early the following morning, they would be dead, found with their throats slit on a bleak stretch of the road to Pudahuel Airport, together with another militant, Santiago Nattino. The next week, at the Avenida Matta school, the girl stops coming to class. Her father no longer drops her off in the morning. Neither does her uncle in the red Chevette. The caretaker doesn't see her crossing herself in front of the statue of the Virgen del Carmen or eating ham and cheese on a roll at recess. The desk at the back of the classroom sits empty now. For some reason, the girl never occupies it again.

II

No one is exactly sure when it happened, but we all remember that coffins and funerals and wreaths were suddenly everywhere and there was no escaping them, because it had all become something like a bad dream. Maybe it had always been that way and we were only just realizing it. Maybe Maldonado was right and we were too young. Maybe we were distracted by all that history homework, all those math tests, all those enactments of battles against the Peruvians. Suddenly things sprang to life in a new way. The classroom opened out to the street, and, desperate and naive, we leaped onto the deck of the enemy ship in a first and final attempt doomed to failure.

Maldonado dreams of the word *degollados*. She sees it printed in the headlines of every newspaper from back then. *Caso Degollados.* Throats slashed. In newsstands, on the dining room table at home, in her mother's hands, in the fat binder on shelf number four in the third aisle of the school library. Maldonado doesn't know what *degollados* means, but she senses that it's something awful and then her dream turns into a nightmare. Fuenzalida dreams of the voice of a newscaster on the radio in her mother's car. The man is talking about a gruesome discovery, that's what he calls it, and he uses the same word, which is new to Fuenzalida too. Zúñiga dreams about the funerals. He says that he was there, he went with his parents and his brother. Acosta remembers a coffin, some place he isn't sure how he got to. There were lots of flowers and candles and people standing in silence, he said. At some point the son of one of the dead men appeared, a kid just like us, in his uniform, with his school crest, and he stood next to the coffin for a long time. Maybe he said something. Acosta can't remember, because he never remembers voices, but the one thing he's sure about is that the kid didn't cry. He didn't cry the whole time he was standing next to his father in that coffin. Zúñiga says that when he got home from the funeral his family was arrested. Zúñiga and his brother were released the next day, but his parents were transferred to some secret location. Donoso and Bustamante got beat up at a student rally. Donoso suffered permanent loss of mobility in his little finger and Bustamante ended up at the Central Hospital with ten stitches in his head. Fuenzalida hears the clamor of a massive march toward the General Cemetery. There are voices shouting and chanting, making demands, praying for the dead. At Riquelme's house, anonymous phone calls begin to come in. A strange voice swears at his mother, who has a job no one knows anything about, because it's secret. The voice tells her that if she keeps fucking around something will happen to her son or her mother. Fuenzalida hears the sound of the crowd tossing flower petals at the hearses, thousands of petals that cover everything like a shower of flyers scattered in the street. Donoso's house was searched by a group of national police agents. They turned it all upside down and broke some furniture but they didn't take anything. Donoso couldn't sleep at night, afraid that a squad would come any minute and take his diaries, his comics, his parents. Fuenzalida hears the footsteps of the crowd advancing with flags and banners. They fill streets, cross bridges, walk on endlessly. We spent a few days looking for Zúñiga's parents but we couldn't find them. They were moved from a police station to some undisclosed location and there was no trace of either of them. One night, as she was leaving work, Riquelme's mother was kidnapped. Twelve hours later she was released. Crosses had been cut into her nipples with a razor blade. Fuenzalida can't remember what funeral she's dreaming of. It might be the one for the brothers from Villa Francia or for the teachers from the Latinoamericano, or for the boy burned to death by a military patrol, or for the priest shot in the settlement of La Victoria, or for the boy riddled with bullets on Calle Bulnes, or for the kidnapped reporter, or for the group assassinated on the Feast of Corpus Christi, or for one of the others, any of the others. Time isn't straightforward, it mixes everything up, shuffles the dead, merges them, separates them out again, advances backward, retreats in reverse, spins like a merry-go-round, like a tiny wheel in a laboratory cage, and traps us in funerals and marches and detentions, leaving us with no assurance of continuity or escape. Whether we were there or not is no longer clear. Whether we took part in it all or not isn't either. But we're left with traces of the dream, like the vestiges of a doomed naval battle. We wake up with smudges of cork beard on our pillows and with the unpleasant feeling of having been assailed by green glow-in-the-dark bullets, by a wooden orthopedic hand.

III

Dear friend, hello! How are you? Better than the last time
I saw you, I hope. You were sick in bed with a fever, and I had
to stand at the door of your room and wave, remember? You're
probably better by now. Things aren't so good here. I don't
know how to tell you this, but maybe the easiest way is to say
I've had some problems, which is why I haven't been answer-
ing the phone or coming to school. The truth is I won't be back.
It's hard for me even to write that. My parents told me yester-
day and I've been crying ever since. I hate leaving without being
able to say good-bye to anyone but I have no choice. My dad had
some problems at work and for security reasons we have to move.
Believe it or not I can't even say where. The truth is they haven't
told me either. All I know is that I'll be going to a German school
so I've got some teachers to catch me up on German. I don't
know how much I'll learn. I'm too sad to concentrate on any-
thing. My mother says not to worry, when things calm down I'll
be able to go back to the school and see you all, but I don't know
whether to believe her or not. For now the best I can do is write
to you and give you all the news I can because I'm not allowed to
tell much more.

Maldonado, you're my best friend and I have a big favor to
ask you. Inside this envelope that my uncle Claudio is bringing
you is a tiny little letter. He doesn't know it's there and neither
does anyone else. It's a secret letter for Zúñiga, because I'm defi-
nitely not allowed to send him anything, so I thought that if I

put it in this envelope you might be able to give it to him. It's
important for him to get it. I heard that his parents were arrested.
I don't know exactly why, but I hope it all works out. Really I do.
Please don't forget to do this for me. Just please don't read it.
I'd die of embarrassment if you did, even though you already
know everything there is to know about us.

Okay, that's all for now. I have faith in you. I'm going to miss
you a lot. All of you. But I promise that when I can be in touch
and tell you more, I will. For now, write me and save the letters
until I send you my new address.

Lots of love. I'm going to miss you so much.

Please don't forget me.

Your friend forever. ★

IV

It all happens on a deserted beach. A place that smells of the sea, where I've come with the rest of my class. Let's go, Zúñiga, I hear them saying. Don't be a slowpoke, catch up. It's a class trip. We're all there, or almost all of us, and we're walking barefoot through the sand, following the seagulls that will lead us to the sea. I'm tired and thirsty, and from where we are, I realize, you can't see the water. You can hear the sound of the waves, you can feel the breeze, but no matter how far we walk we never get anywhere. Maybe there's no sea. Maybe it's just an idea, a fantasy.

Acosta and Bustamante sing an annoying song while we walk. Their voices are shrill, like vultures, but nobody complains, we all keep moving under the sun, roasting our backs, an army of little soldiers trying to reach some strategic location. Maybe we're on a mission and all of this is part of a war, an important battle, but the truth is we don't know. We just keep walking under the illusion that if we keep going, eventually we'll be able to get our feet wet.

After a while, or maybe not so long, Riquelme brings us to an abrupt halt. The march stops and he speaks as if he's in charge, though he isn't. He says that this is as far as we're going, because a big sand pool has suddenly appeared at his feet. We couldn't see it from a distance, but now here it is. It's a hole full of seawater. It isn't the sea, it's a hole in the middle of the beach and we have to get in before a wave hits it or the sun dries up its walls and the whole thing collapses. Someone has built it for us. There are brightly colored plastic shovels and buckets and rakes scattered on the sand. We don't question any of this, because in dreams nobody questions things, and suddenly we're all naked, swimming in the sand pool. Don't be chicken, Zúñiga, jump in, they call, and I do, I get in and duck under. We splash around happily, dunking each other, diving. Riquelme is like a duck in the water, he's in and out and splashing us all, and it's a happy moment, our one happy moment, because the heat has lifted, because we aren't thinking about the sea or the war anymore, because Acosta and Bustamante have stopped shrieking like vultures, because finally we have this little sandpit where we can swim for a while.

In the dream I think about the Battle of Concepción. At some point we studied it in history class. In the dream I remember parts of the class, the parts I want to remember. The teacher with a piece of chalk in her hand writing names and dates on the board. The end of a war, I think. The War of the Pacific, Chile's endless struggle with Peru and Bolivia. Skirmishes under the sun, in the middle of the desert. The idea of an ambush, a trap, and the certainty that there were dead children in this battle. Probably they weren't so little. Probably they were like us, an army of adolescents, cheap cannon fodder with crap names, from a shitty school, with no hallowed traditions or view of the mountains, with no foreign languages for protection, dark-skinned kids jumping into the pool without life vests, bare-assed, preparing the terrain for others, always others. Little tin soldiers splashing in this fake sea, no clue what battle they're fighting.

The plug, shouts Donoso. The plug. Somebody pulled the plug.

The sand is swirling. Everything is draining. There's a hole in the bottom of the pool and it's beginning to swallow up my classmates. It swallows Bustamante. It swallows Fuenzalida. It swallows Maldonado. And I hear screams and the dream turns dangerous and I'm scared. I knew I shouldn't have jumped into the water. Who pulled the plug? shouts Riquelme, and before his shout drowns in my ears I watch the hole swallow him up too. Riquelme is gone. I can't hear his voice or anybody else's. I can't see their naked bodies splashing in the water. No one is left. Everybody has gone down the dark drain, who knows where. And then I struggle, I try not to fall, I flail and cling to the walls of sand, but the current is stronger than I am and it sucks me down and the walls collapse and there I go. My feet are in the hole, my legs, my thighs, my chest, my body, and before I disappear I see her high up on the edge with the plug in her hands.

She's naked.

She looks pretty. She always looks pretty.

Her black hair soaked with seawater, that faint scent of gum.

Forgive me, Zúñiga, she says. Please, forgive me.

V

Santiago de Chile. 1994. Nine years after the fact, the Chilean justice system delivers its first ruling on the kidnapping and murder of communist militants José Manuel Parada, Manuel Guerrero, and Santiago Nattino, in what up until now has been known as the Caso Degollados. The officers who committed the crime are sentenced to life in prison. On the same television screen where we used to play *Space Invaders*, we see the national police agents guilty of the murders. Six officers were involved. They appear in plain sight. Their faces scroll across the screen one after the other.

Riquelme is the first of us to recognize him. His face, ten years older, tells Riquelme nothing, but the wooden hand in a black glove does. It's a real hand, not the glow-in-the-dark green fantasy that chases Riquelme in his dreams. Next to him is Uncle Claudio of the red Chevy. El Pegaso, they call him. He says that he was following the orders of his superior, Don Guillermo González Betancourt. He states that he stabbed one of the three men as his superior watched from the car, a red Chevette. All of us see him on the television screen. In some strange way we tune in to the same image at the same time.

VI

Our paper ship begins to take on water.
We tumble onto the white sheet and go under.
We lie there submerged.
Not knowing how to wake up.

Game Over

I

Santiago de Chile. 1991. One October morning, national police lieutenant Félix Sazo Sepúlveda enters the Crowne Plaza hotel in the center of Santiago. The lieutenant rapidly approaches the Avis rent-a-car counter, behind which stands twenty-one-year-old Estrella González Jepssen, mother of his young son. Estrella is attending to a customer when Lieutenant Sazo aims his service revolver at her. They've been separated for some time. The lieutenant has struggled to accept the fact of their separation. That's why he's been following her, harassing her over the phone, threatening her the way you'd threaten an enemy, an alien, a communist teacher. Estrella, he shouts. Our classmate scarcely has time to look at him before she's struck by two bullets in the chest, one in the head, and a fourth in the back.

Like a little Martian she flies apart into colored lights.

On-screen the score on the board goes up one hundred points.

And still the record stands.

Estrella collapses in the fetal position, dying instantly. Police lieutenant Félix Sazo immediately shoots himself twice in the head with his smoking service revolver and falls to the ground.

We didn't dream any of this.

We read it in the crime pages of a newspaper found on the fourth shelf of the third aisle in the school library.

II

I wake up.

She's sitting on my bed.

I feel the weight of her body next to mine.

Zúñiga, she says, you survived. I hear her over the white noise of the television, which is still on. It's late. I know I'm dreaming, but her voice in my ear is as real as the weight of her body. It's her. I can see her by the light of the television screen. She's naked and wet. Her black hair tangled from the sand and salt. Her pubic hair too. Your parents? she asks me. Did they ever let them go? I'm afraid to talk, because I don't want her to disappear. They're fine, I manage to say. Old and deaf, but fine. She smiles and hands me the letter that never reached me. It's written on graph paper from a math notebook. I smell the scent of gum in her hair when she comes close. The television screen announces a new day's programming. It begins with the national anthem and pictures of the whole country from Arica to Punta Arenas.

I wake up again.

There's no television. There's no letter.

I'm alone and I'm eons older.

III

We're standing one after another in a long line down the middle of the street. Next to us is another long line, and another, and another. We make a perfect square, a kind of game board. We're pieces in a game that we don't know how to stop playing. We spread out, each of us resting a right arm on the shoulder of the classmate ahead to mark the perfect distance between us. Our uniforms neat. Top button of the shirt fastened, tie knotted, dark jumper below the knee, blue socks pulled up, pants perfectly ironed, school crest sewn on at proper chest height, no threads dangling, shoes freshly shined. Around us the street is silent and empty. There are no cars, no buses, no people. Just us and this guerrilla logic that we can't wake up from. We could take attendance, starting with Acosta and moving on to Bustamante, then Donoso, but it's not necessary. We're all here. We were scheduled to meet here. We've risen from our sheets and mattresses scattered around the city to arrive precisely on time. As always, the dream summons us.

A pay phone rings on the street, right by the school entrance.

We look at each other. Somehow we've been expecting this call.

Fuenzalida steps forward. She's an expert in voices, so she'll have no trouble recognizing who's speaking. Hello? Somehow we know that it's a female voice on the phone.

Fuenzalida doesn't say a word, but we can tell who it is from the look she gives us. A woman or a child is breathing nervously at the other end of the line, waiting for a reply. Fuenzalida realizes this telephone call is fated. We have to take it. Without hesitating for a second, she answers and starts to talk. Standing in the street, uncomfortable in our old uniforms, now too tight and faded, we listen attentively.

Santiago de Chile, April 2013

Acknowledgments

On the threshold of the dream, I thank Maldonado.

For her letters, her memories, and her friendship,
bulletproof and time-tested.

Nona Fernández was born in Santiago, Chile, in 1971. She is an actress and writer, and has published two plays, a collection of short stories, and six novels. In 2016 she was awarded the Premio Sor Juana Inés de la Cruz. Her books have been translated into French, Italian, German, and English.

Natasha Wimmer is the translator of nine books by Roberto Bolaño, including *The Savage Detectives* and *2666*. Her most recent translations are Bolaño's *The Spirit of Science Fiction* and *Sudden Death*, by Álvaro Enrigue. She lives in Brooklyn with her husband and two children.

The text of *Space Invaders* is set in Arno Pro.
Book design by Rachel Holscher.
Composition by Bookmobile Design and Digital Publisher
Services, Minneapolis, Minnesota.
Manufactured by Versa Press on acid-free,
30 percent postconsumer wastepaper.